# HOT ON THE TRAIL IN
# ANCIENT EGYPT

This book is for my daughter, Lia Grainger, who once did a school project on the Sphinx and has been in love with all things Egyptian ever since — L.B.

For Phil and Rosemary, who inspire me with their love of travel to exotic places — B.S.

Acknowledgments

I'm very grateful for the help of Dr. Julie Anderson, Curator, Ancient Egypt and Sudan, British Museum, London, and Dr. Ronald J. Leprohon, Professor of Egyptology, University of Toronto, both of whom kindly reviewed this book for accuracy and provided invaluable advice. Any errors or inaccuracies in the text are my own.

Huge thanks to Valerie Wyatt, my original editor, for making this book's evolution such a pleasure — and further thanks to the great team at Kids Can Press: Jennifer Stokes, Katie Scott, Yvette Ghione, Julia Naimska, Katie Gray, Olga Kidisevic and Genie MacLeod. Kudos also to Bill Slavin for bringing the Binkertons so splendidly to life on the page.

I am grateful as well to friend and fellow writer Deborah Hodge for her nonfiction wisdom, and to Emily McLellan and Jeremie Lauck Stephenson for their age-appropriate feedback. My daughters (Lia and Tess) provided laughs, ideas and support and my friend Anna Koeller helped with critiques and dog walks. Finally, I would like to say a belated thank-you to my high school history teacher. Great work, Mr. Visch — you made it fun!

Kids Can Press gratefully acknowledges the financial support of the Government of Ontario, through the Ontario Media Development Corporation; the Ontario Arts Council; the Canada Council for the Arts; and the Government of Canada, through the CBF, for our publishing activity.

Published in Canada and the U.S. by Kids Can Press Ltd.
25 Dockside Drive, Toronto, ON  M5A 0B5

Kids Can Press is a Corus Entertainment Inc. company

www.kidscanpress.com

The artwork in this book was rendered in pen and ink and watercolor.
The text is set in Adobe Jenson Pro and Rainier.

Edited by Valerie Wyatt
Designed by Julia Naimska

Printed and bound in Buji, Shenzhen, China, in 10/2017 by WKT Company

CM 18 0 9 8 7 6 5 4 3 2 1

**Library and Archives Canada Cataloguing in Publication**

Bailey, Linda, 1948–, author
Hot on the trail in ancient Egypt / written by Linda Bailey ; illustrated by Bill Slavin.

(The time travel guides)
ISBN 978-1-77138-985-3 (softcover)

1. Time travel — Comic books, strips, etc. 2. Time travel — Juvenile fiction. 3. Egypt, Ancient — Comic books, strips, etc. 4. Egypt, Ancient — Juvenile fiction. 5. Graphic novels.  I. Slavin, Bill, illustrator  II. Title.

PN6733.B35H68 2018       j741.5'971       C2017-903963-6

# HOT ON THE TRAIL IN
# ANCIENT EGYPT

Written by Linda Bailey

Illustrated by Bill Slavin

Kids Can Press

The Binkerton twins were bored. Seriously, horribly, fall-right-over-and-go-to-sleep bored.

All their friends had gone away on exciting summer holidays — to Disneyland, to the Rockies, to scuba diving camp. The only place Josh and Emma had gone was around the block ... and around ... and around. They had to take their little sister, Libby, with them.

Each time they passed the Good Times Travel Agency, they walked a little faster — and no wonder! Good Times was dark. It was creepy. It was grotty and grimy and grungy. There were cobwebs as big as your *mother* in there.

So the Binkertons always hurried past ... until the day that Libby ran inside.

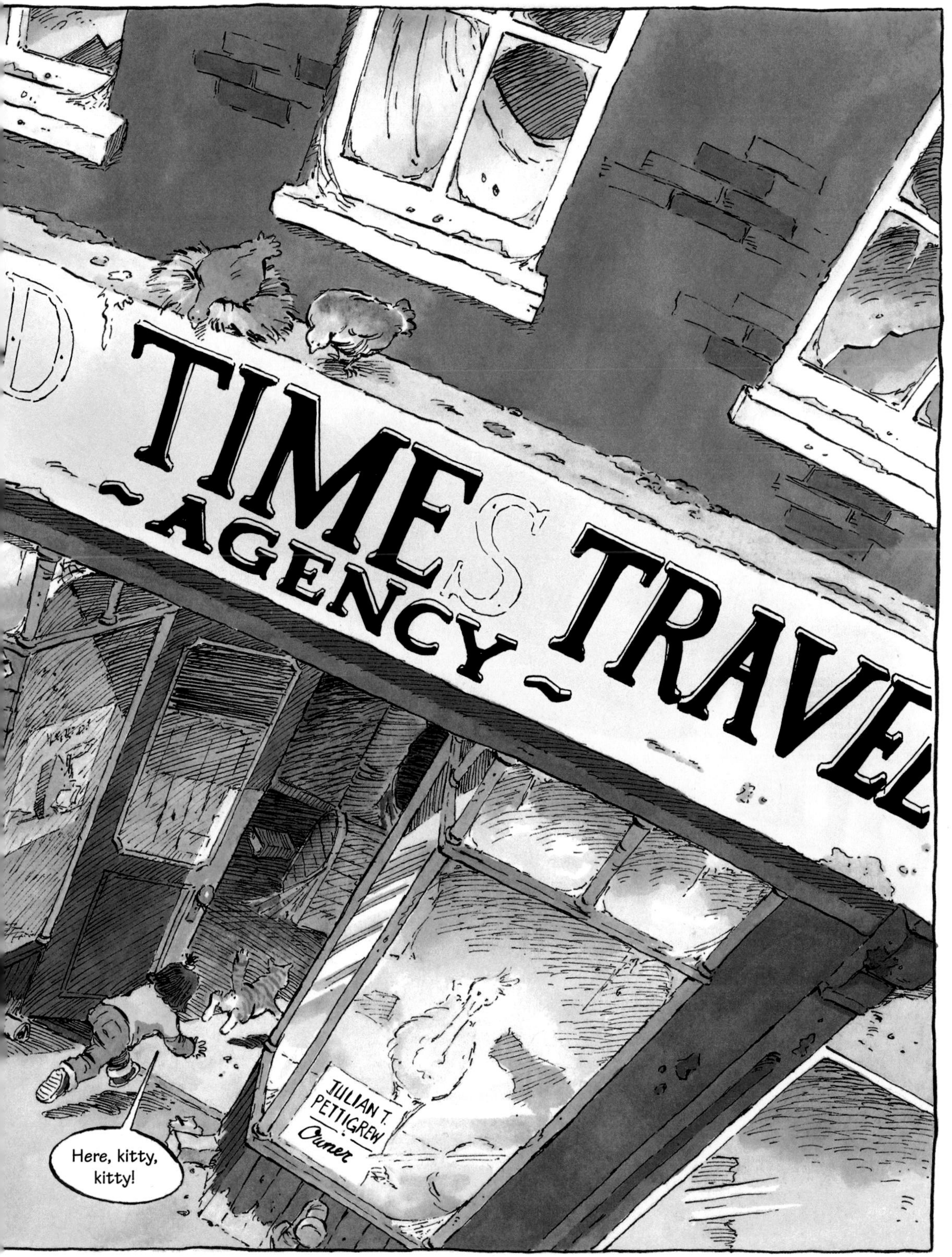
TIMES TRAVEL
~AGENCY~
JULIAN T. PETTIGREW
Owner
Here, kitty, kitty!

Julian T. Pettigrew, the owner, glanced up as they entered. He looked every bit as peculiar as his shop.

Customers? Hmmm …

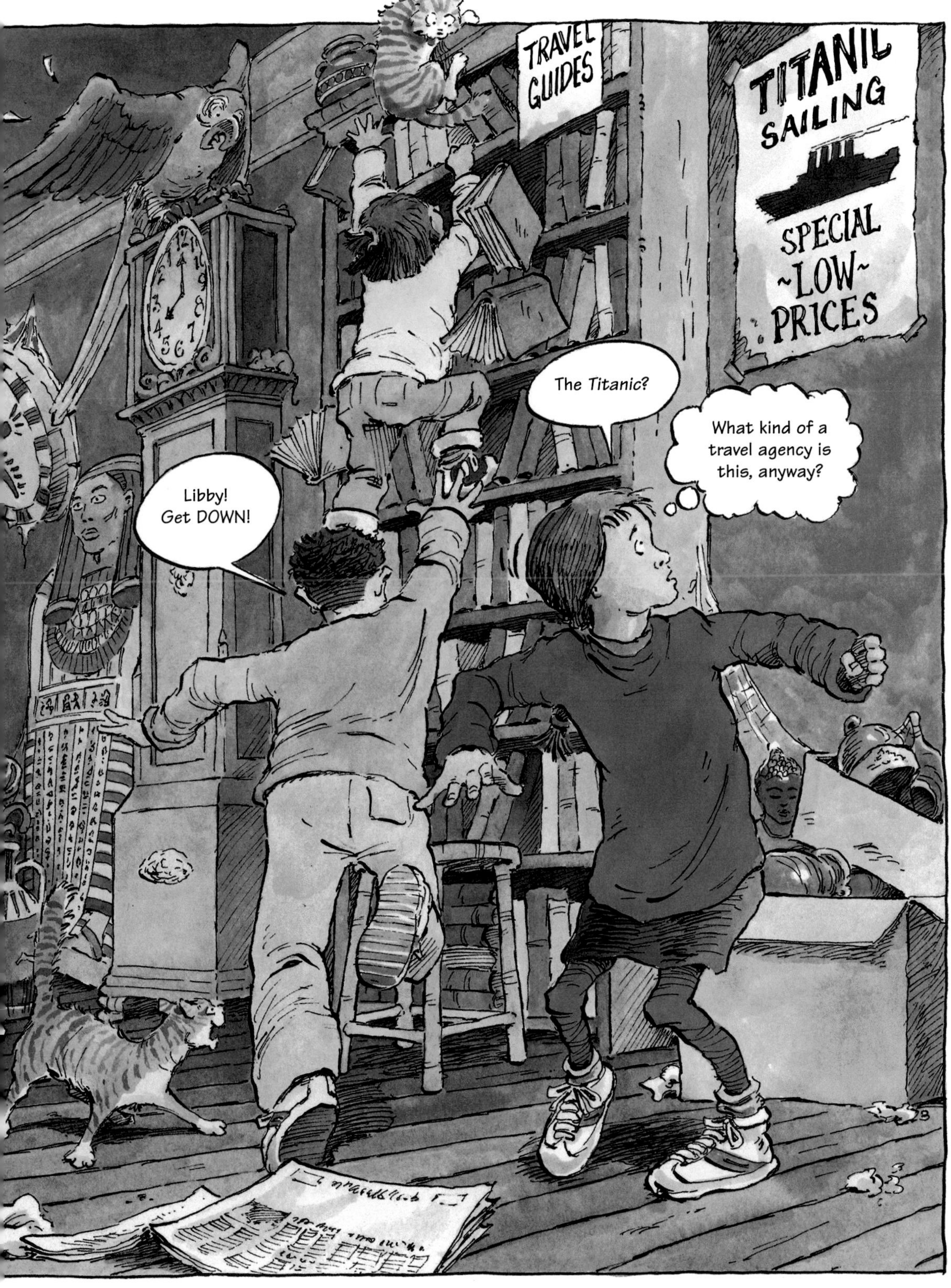
TRAVEL GUIDES
TITANIC SAILING
SPECIAL ~LOW~ PRICES
The *Titanic*?
What kind of a travel agency is this, anyway?
Libby! Get DOWN!

If it had been up to Emma, the Binkertons would have been out of there in two seconds flat. But Libby, as usual, made things difficult.

Oh my! We haven't had a customer since ...

1918? 1981? 1819?

We're not customers, sir. We're —

Good kitty.

Oww! LIB-BEE!!

The more Emma saw of the travel agency, and the more she heard from Julian T. Pettigrew — the more nervous she got.

What a weird old book.

Ancient Egypt? Excellent choice! You'll love it there!

Love it where? What do you mean?

Even though Emma had never seen Pettigrew's weird old book before, she had a very strange feeling about it — so strange that she tried to keep her brother from opening it. She *almost* succeeded.

Josh! DON'T!

But *almost* wasn't quite good enough. There was a terrible, wonderful flash and ...

Have a good time!

... in one brief moment, everything changed!

Wh-what? Where are we?

Oh ... my ... gosh.

## JULIAN T. PETTIGREW'S PERSONAL GUIDE TO ANCIENT EGYPT

WELCOME to ancient Egypt! And congratulations on picking this sunny, hot spot for your holiday. You've chosen a terrific time — around 2500 BCE.

Did you bring an umbrella? If so, you can dump it right now. It almost never rains in ancient Egypt. In fact, most of the land around here is desert. The only reason it isn't *all* desert is — the Nile River.

Ah ... the Nile. What a magnificent river it is! Why? Because without the Nile, nothing else in ancient Egypt would be possible. It flows north from the mountains in Africa through the desert to the sea, providing life-giving water to the land on each side.

It took Emma only seconds to figure out what had happened — the Binkertons had traveled through time.

Ancient Egypt, Josh! It says so right here.

After a careful look at the Guidebook, Emma figured out something else. They were stuck there! They couldn't go home until they had read every word of *Pettigrew's Personal Guide to Ancient Egypt.*

Well, we *wanted* a holiday.

Yes, but not 4500 years away from home!

Imagine an oasis 1000 km (600 mi.) long and only a few kilometers (or miles) wide, and you'll have a pretty good idea of the shape of ancient Egypt. See for yourself on the map. It's the long, skinny green bit.

Mediterranean Sea

Nile River

Western Desert

Red Sea

Eastern Desert

You're lucky to show up at flood time. Once a year, from July to October, the Nile overflows its banks and floods the surrounding fields. This is called the Inundation. People here love it, and so they should. When the river goes down again, it leaves behind a thick layer of fertile mud — great for growing crops of all kinds.

In the meantime, the countryside can get a little ... well ... damp.

Wading around in the muddy waters of the Nile wasn't going to get the Binkertons anywhere. So they headed for higher ground — and their first real, live Egyptians.

At least, the Binkertons *hoped* they were alive.

She doesn't look 4500 years old.

My name is Aneksi. Welcome to my home.

## Ancient Egyptian Homes

If you want to see a typical Egyptian home, drop in on a farming family. Most ancient Egyptians are peasant-farmers. They live in small villages along the Nile and grow crops in the rich black soil left by the flood. They build their houses on high ground where the flood doesn't reach.

Building a house in ancient Egypt is easy. Even *you* could do it. All you need is mud, and there's plenty of that around. Just mix it with straw and put it into molds. Let it bake in the sun and — presto! — mud bricks. The Egyptians plaster these bricks together to make houses. The flat roofs are used as extra living space. The windows are high and small to keep the house cool. Many houses are painted white inside and out.

The houses of ordinary people are small and don't have a lot of furniture — a few stools or small tables and mats. Wood is scarce here, so wooden furniture is expensive.

Aneksi turned out to be very much alive — and friendly, too. The Binkertons relaxed. They even accepted Aneksi's invitation to come inside for refreshments.

## Food and Drink

The most important food here is bread. Careful — it may have bits of sand and grit in it. That's because the grain for the flour is ground between two flat rocks. Bits of stone sometimes rub off. Many Egyptians have worn-down teeth from chomping on sand.

Perhaps you'd rather try some delicious fresh fruit. Figs, perhaps? Grapes, dates, pomegranates? They're all picked locally.

For drinks, try the national beverage — beer! It's made from half-cooked bread and river water, and it's thick, dark and sometimes a bit lumpy. You're *supposed* to strain it well before serving, but not everyone does.

## Egyptian Clothing

Because it's so hot here, clothing is simple. It's almost always white and made out of linen. If you're a man, you'll put on a loincloth or kilt (short skirt). Women wear simple, straight dresses. Young children wear … very little. People generally go barefoot here, but may wear sandals if they have them.

Just as Emma was trying to figure out a polite way to say that they didn't drink beer, a group of official-looking men arrived. They had come to get Aneksi's brother, Hapu, to take him to work for the king.

But Hapu wasn't there — and Josh was! Josh tried to explain that they were getting the wrong guy ...

## Ancient Egyptian Society

If you had to pick a job in ancient Egypt, a good choice would be king. The king owns all the land. He owns everything in it. He gets to run the country, too. Everyone obeys his commands without question. To the ancient Egyptians, he isn't just a king — he's also a living god. The people here believe he's the son of Re, their sun god. They believe he can speak directly to the gods and ask for good floods and rich crops.

Other jobs in ancient Egypt aren't quite as good as king. Below him are the nobles and officials, who help him rule. Below them are the temple priests and scribes, who are respected because they can read and write. A step lower are the skilled craftsmen. Down at the bottom are the farmers and laborers. Most people in ancient Egypt are at the bottom of the society — where there's plenty of room!

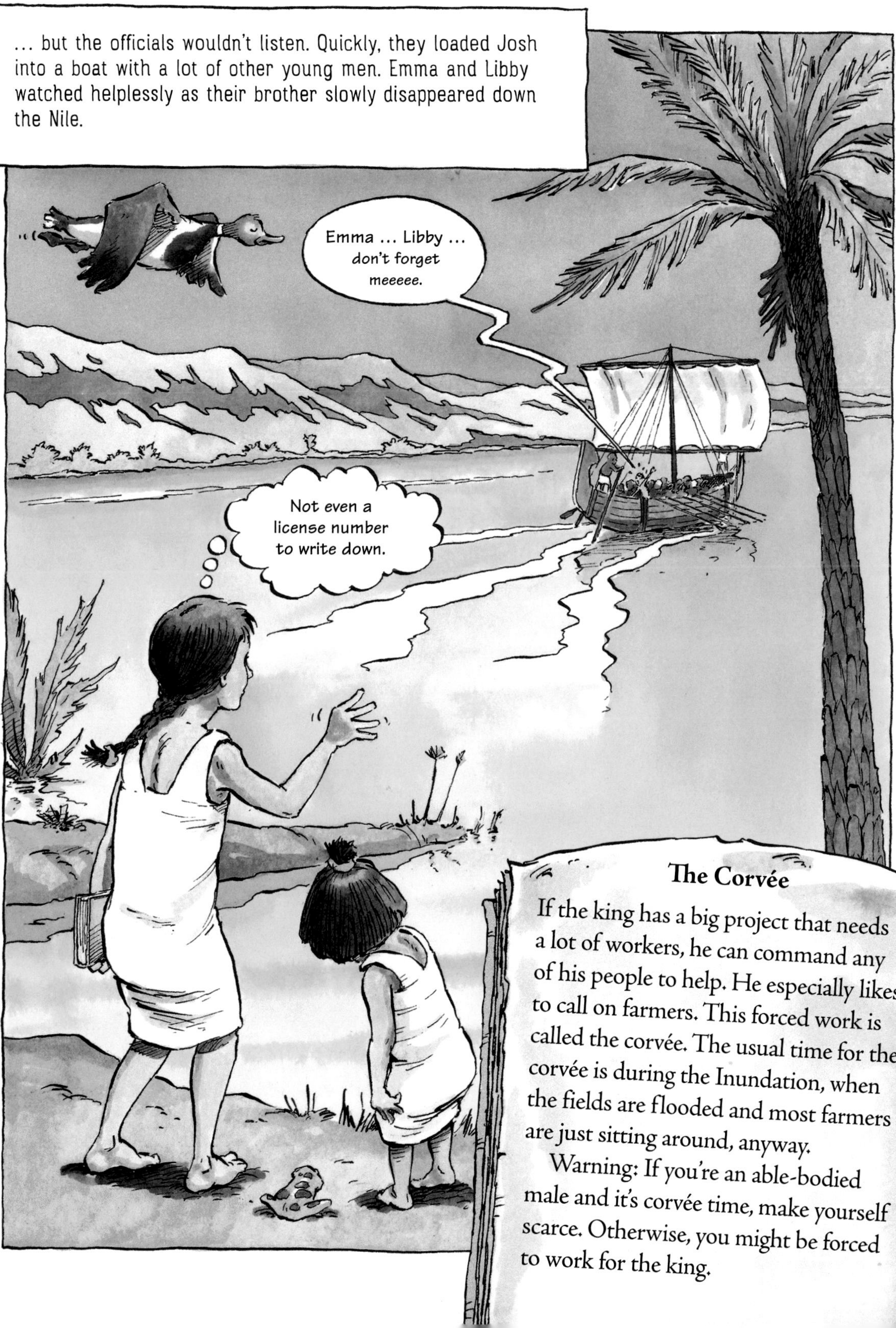
... but the officials wouldn't listen. Quickly, they loaded Josh into a boat with a lot of other young men. Emma and Libby watched helplessly as their brother slowly disappeared down the Nile.
Emma ... Libby ... don't forget meeeee.
Not even a license number to write down.

## The Corvée

If the king has a big project that needs a lot of workers, he can command any of his people to help. He especially likes to call on farmers. This forced work is called the corvée. The usual time for the corvée is during the Inundation, when the fields are flooded and most farmers are just sitting around, anyway.

Warning: If you're an able-bodied male and it's corvée time, make yourself scarce. Otherwise, you might be forced to work for the king.

Emma felt sick. Josh wasn't perfect — far from it — but he was the only twin brother she had! She and Libby set out after him. Eventually, they came to a bustling settlement beside the Nile. Emma was positive they would find Josh there.

We'll find him if we have to take this town apart, brick by brick.

Find-Joshy, find-Joshy, find —

Over the next few hours, the two girls dragged themselves from one end of town to another, searching for their brother. They knocked on doors and stopped strangers in the street. They questioned craftsmen selling their wares.

Joshy?

He has brown eyes and — no, I have sandals at home, thank you!

## An Egyptian Town

Try to spend at least some of your holiday in one of the larger towns along the Nile. Towns are centers of trade and government. They're also great places for people-watching. The streets, especially in the poorer sections, are narrow and crowded with people going about their business. If you feel like shopping, look for craftsmen selling pottery, sandals, reed mats and other products.

Notice a nasty smell or two? Try to ignore it. There's no garbage pickup here and no sewer system either, and what with the heat …

They spoke to priests at a temple.

He's about this tall and —

Out! Out!

## Temples and Gods

Religious temples are quiet and peaceful, but don't expect to be invited inside. An Egyptian temple is like a private palace for a god to live in. The god is represented by a statue, kept in a shrine. The statue is washed, dressed and even fed by temple priests. It doesn't actually *eat* the food, of course. (Fortunately, the priests have good appetites.)

The ancient Egyptians believe in hundreds of different gods. Not all have great temples. Some are worshiped only in certain parts of the country. Others are household spirits thought to help with everyday problems. Many Egyptian gods are shown in animal form — the crocodile, the hawk, the lion, the hippopotamus and so on.

Hour after hour, Emma and Libby searched, while the hot Egyptian sun beat down on their backs. By the end of the day, the girls were tired, hungry and parched with thirst.

When they were offered food and lodging — in exchange for work — they had no choice but to accept. A wealthy family giving a party was short of servants. Emma was a little shocked by the party entertainment ...

... but Libby leaped right in.

Hey, Emma! Watch me.

I am *never* taking her anywhere again!

## A Banquet

If you're hanging around with wealthy Egyptians, you may be invited to a banquet. Don't be shy. Put some flowers around your neck and join right in!

The food's terrific. There's roast goose, duck and quail served with fresh vegetables — onions, leeks, beans, cucumbers and lettuce. And lucky you! Beef is on the menu. Only wealthy people can afford this luxury. If you have a sweet tooth, look for honey cakes, figs and other fresh fruit. For drinks, most guests wash their food down with wine — sometimes too *much* wine.

Don't forget your table manners. Squat or sit close to the table. Sit with the men if you're male, or the women if you're female. Use your fingers to eat — BUT NOT ALL OF THEM! Only three fingers of your right hand.

The best part of a banquet is the entertainment. The ancient Egyptians adore music. Feel free to clap along with the flutes, harps, drums, rattles — and dancing girls! The dancers twist and bend like gymnasts. They even do acrobatic stunts. (Perhaps it helps that they don't wear too many clothes.)

Finished eating? Try a game of senet. It's a quiet board game and very popular here.

Over the next few days, Emma and Libby continued to work for the Egyptian family while spending every spare moment searching for Josh. When one of the other servants told them about a teacher "who knows many things," they tracked the man down at his school.

L-I-B-B-Y.
Libby!

?

It is true —
I know many
things.

Unfortunately, the teacher didn't know the one thing that mattered to Emma and Libby.

C-A-T.
Cat!

... and after the
great King Djoser
came Sekhemkhet and
Khaba, followed by the
long reign of King
Huni and ...

Where's the off
button?

?

Emma had one uncomfortable moment when the teacher noticed the Guidebook and wanted a closer look. But she quickly distracted him by asking about *his* books.

That's a book?

... and in the reign of the great King Sneferu, in the time of the flood ...

Help?

I-J-I-P-T. Egypt!

Mrowp?

## Learning and Schools

Most learning goes on at home. Boys learn the same work as their fathers — fishing, farming, craftwork and so on. Girls are taught to run a household by their mothers.

Some boys (and a few privileged girls) are taught reading, writing and math in small schools. Warning: If you visit a school, be careful around the teacher — especially if he has a big stick in his hand! There's an old Egyptian saying: "A boy's ears are on his back. He listens best when he is beaten."

Some hardworking boys become scribes (men trained to write letters, record information and help run the government). Scribes can become priests or army officers — or even prime minister. It's a great honor to be a scribe — and

easier than farming out in the hot sun!

Perhaps you'd like to learn the ancient Egyptian alphabet while you're here. How hard could it be? Well ... quite hard, actually. It's a kind of picture-writing called hieroglyphics, and it has more than 700 different symbols.

To try it, you'll need a reed brush and some ink made from soot. Practice on bits of broken pottery (ostraca). Scrolls of paper (papyrus) are made from thin strips of reeds pounded together. But they're *much* too precious to waste on students.

As time passed with no word of Josh, Emma got more and more anxious. At night, she lay awake worrying.

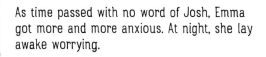

How will I ever explain to Mom and Dad?

She worried in the daytime, too — mostly about how to keep her sister out of trouble!

LIB-BEE! What are you DOING?

### Sleeping in Ancient Egypt

Rich Egyptians sleep on wooden-framed beds. Poorer people sleep on mats or on clay platforms covered in matting. To beat the heat, you may want to bed down, Egyptian-style, on the roof. Aaah … feel that breeze? Very cool!

Looking for a pillow? Try an ancient Egyptian headrest. They're made of wood, ivory or stone, and they *look* like instruments of torture. They can come in handy, though, for keeping your head off the ground — especially when scorpions or snakes wander by.

### Makeup and Jewelry

If you want to look your best in Egypt, makeup is just the thing. Start by outlining your eyes with black kohl and green eye paint. Stain your fingernails with henna. Dab yourself with scented oils. (In ancient Egypt, it's important to smell nice.)

Next put on jewelry — colored beads perhaps, or a gold bracelet or amulet (magic charm) to ward off evil spirits. Finish your new look with a wig. People here keep their hair short and wear wigs on special occasions.

There! You're gorgeous.

Libby quickly made friends with the local children. She fit in well — in Emma's opinion, a little *too* well.

Put your clothes back on, Libby!

WHYYYYY?

One day, Libby and her new friends went off to swim in the river. Emma was relieved ... until she read the next page in Pettigrew's Guidebook.

Crocodiles? In the Nile? Oh my gosh ... LIBBY!

### Egyptian Children

Young children in ancient Egypt wear very few clothes. Actually ... none. After all, it *is* very hot. You may notice an odd hairstyle on the boys. It's called a "lock of youth." Boys wear it till they're ten or twelve.

Egyptian children have simple homemade dolls, tops and pull-toys. They love to wrestle and play tug-of-war and ball games. Also, living beside the Nile, they like to go swimming. It's too bad there are crocodiles. But don't worry. Only a *few* children get eaten.

Running as hard as she could, Emma managed — just barely — to snatch her little sister from the jaws of death.

Here, boy.

LIB-BEEE! NO!

Emma collapsed, exhausted, on the riverbank. That's where she noticed ... the boats.

Maybe someone here has seen him!

Joshy?

## Hunting and Fishing

The Nile is full of food — if you can catch it! Try fishing with spears, nets, or hooks and lines. Or go after some of the waterfowl that live in the marshy areas — ducks, geese, herons or cranes. Ancient Egyptians trap these birds in nets or use throw-sticks to bring them down.

If you feel like taking your life in your hands, you could try hippo-hunting. Join some other hunters in a small boat. Sneak up on a huge hippopotamus. Throw a spear at it. Keep in mind that the hippopotamus will *not* like this!

On second thought, forget hippo-hunting.

Walking beside the river, the girls finally got a lucky break. Some men building a papyrus boat had seen Josh only two days before.

Complains a lot, right?

He's downriver, at the work site.

The problem now was — how to travel on the Nile? But watching the men had given Emma an idea. Why couldn't she and Libby build their own boat?

Will it float, Emma?

Of course.

## Travel on the Nile

The Nile is Egypt's great highway. All you need is a boat! If you want to go north, just drift with the current. To go south, put up a sail and let the wind carry you. (Paddles and poles help, too.) Watch for other boats — fishing boats, cargo boats, pleasure boats and huge barges. Most common of all are small boats made from papyrus reeds.

## How to Build a Papyrus Boat

Cut down some papyrus reeds. (You'll find them growing beside the river.) Lash them together in bundles. Tie them tightly, or they won't be waterproof. Point the ends up. Ready? Away you go!

(P.S. You *can* swim, can't you?)

As Emma and Libby floated down the great Egyptian highway, they saw their first pyramids. Not all of them were perfect.

Well, it's a start.

Better.

Bingo!

## Pyramids

If there's one thing you *must* see in ancient Egypt, it's the pyramids.

They're huge! They're awesome! And they're built with just one purpose — as tombs for Egyptian kings. The ancient Egyptians believe that the king lives on after death. But he can only do this if his soul (Ba) and his life force (Ka) can return to his dead body when they need to. That's why, when a king dies, his body is preserved in a lifelike condition and placed in a burial chamber deep inside or beneath a pyramid.

It took the Egyptians a few generations to figure out how to build pyramids.

At first, they just put the king's body in a mastaba (a rectangle made of mud bricks with a burial chamber underneath).

Then they piled up a few mastabas to make a step pyramid with six "steps."

Meanwhile, farther down the Nile, Josh had been given a very big job. In fact, in the whole history of the family, no Binkerton had *ever* been given such a big job.

Hey, Mr. Pettigrew! Joke's over. Can I go home now?

After that came a bent pyramid. This was *almost* right.

Finally … success! A true pyramid shape.

Next, the Egyptians decided to make some really *big* pyramids. How big? Would you believe as tall as a forty-story skyscraper? Would you believe more than 2 million limestone blocks? Would you believe over 6 million tonnes (tons) of rock? That's big!

Imagine building something that huge with no machinery. No bulldozers, no cranes, no wheels — just human muscle! Thousands of workers are needed to do the job — as many as 4000 all year round, plus 20 000 or 30 000 extra during flood season. Even with all those workers, it can take twenty years — or more — to build a pyramid.

What does all this mean to you? Well, if you've "volunteered" to help, you could be here for a *long* time.

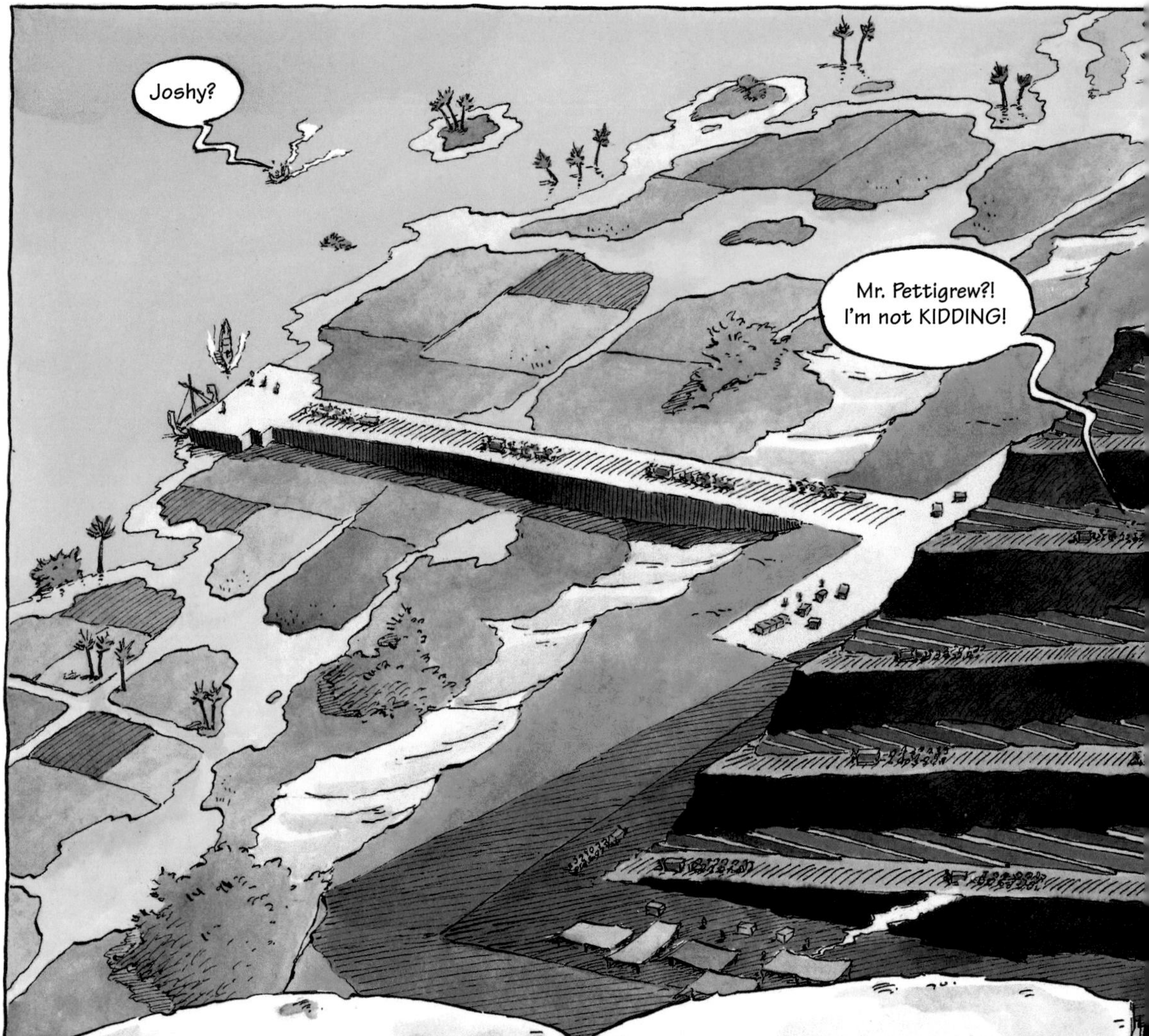
Joshy?
Mr. Pettigrew?! I'm not KIDDING!

## How to Build a Pyramid (Just in Case They Put You in Charge)

1. Pick a good spot — on the west side of the Nile, above the flood line and close to a large deposit of limestone.
2. Make the spot level. Then mark out the four sides of the pyramid to face north, south, east and west.
3. Quarry the limestone. (Cut large blocks out of the ground, using simple tools made of copper, wood or stone.)
4. Bring the limestone blocks to the spot you picked. (Hint: This is the *hard* part.) Put ropes around them and drag them on sleds. Use logs and oil or water to make a good sliding path. (Blocks from far away will have to be dragged to the river, floated on a barge and *then* dragged to the site.)

5. Build the pyramid. (Hint: This is the *really* hard part.) After the first layer of stone, you will have to build ramps so that you can drag the heavy blocks … up … hill!

6. Keep building. Keep building. Keep building. Keep building.

7. Oops! Did you remember to dig a burial chamber underneath the pyramid first? Did you leave space for a passage to the chamber?

8. Put a special pyramid-shaped stone (a capstone) on top.

9. Smooth and polish the shiny white limestone on the outside so the pyramid will gleam in the sun.

10. Take down the ramps. Oh, my! Isn't it lovely? Aren't you proud?

Like the other pyramid workers, Josh was getting paid for his work. But he wasn't impressed with the wages.

He complained to his fellow workers, but they weren't very sympathetic.

Onions? I'm knocking myself out for onions?

It is our duty to build the king's tomb.

He will look after us in the afterlife.

We are the Strong Gang!

Sigh!

**Special Tips for Pyramid Workers**

* Watch out for heatstroke!
* Watch out for insects!
* Don't get sunburned!
* Avoid rope burn!
* Drink plenty of water!
* Try not to get crushed!

* Don't fall off the pyramid!
* BE CAREFUL!
Whew! If you make it through the day, you can go collect your wages — bread, beer, onions and clothing. (And maybe a helping of meat.) Enjoy!

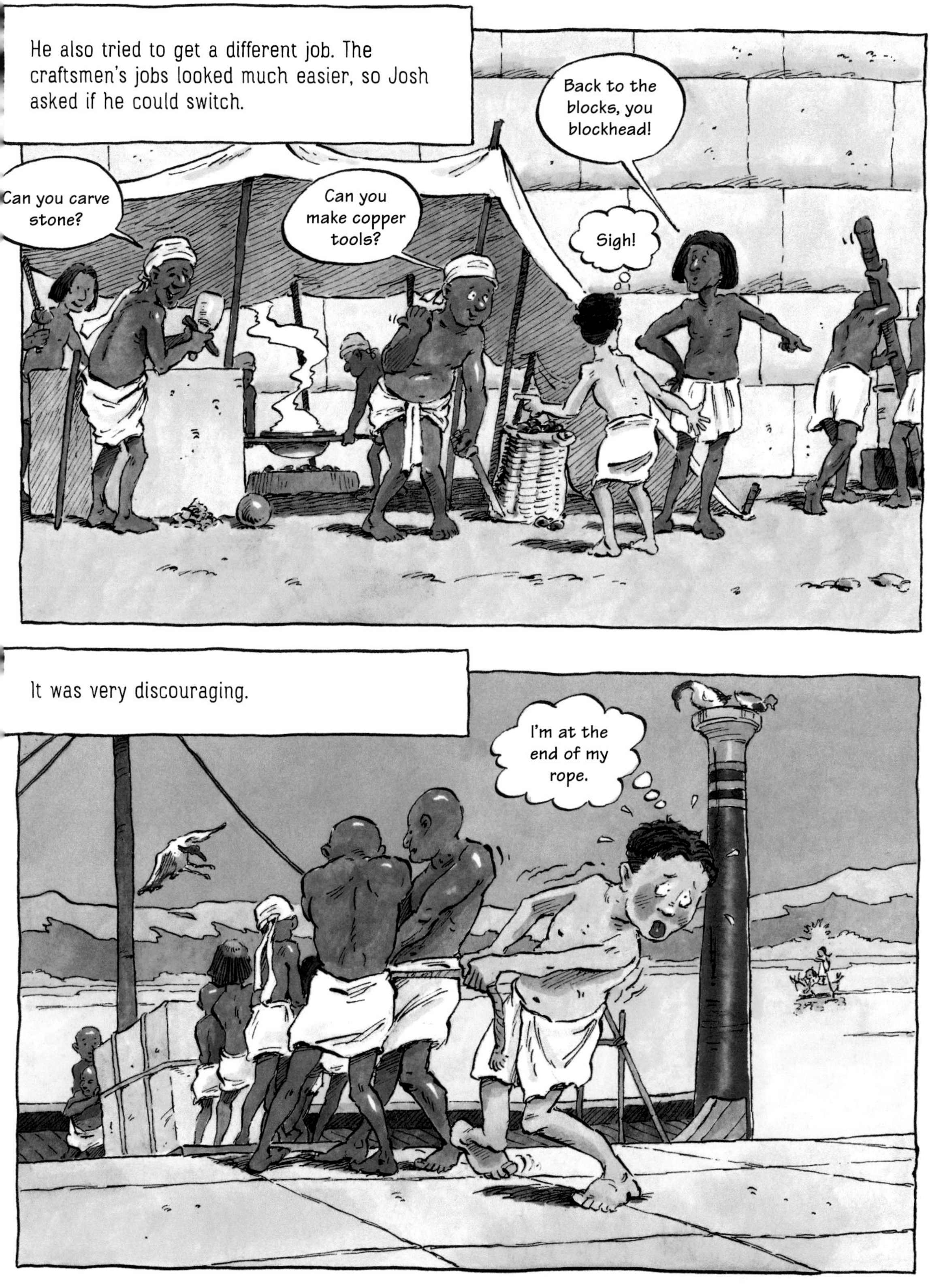
He also tried to get a different job. The craftsmen's jobs looked much easier, so Josh asked if he could switch.
Can you carve stone?
Can you make copper tools?
Sigh!
Back to the blocks, you blockhead!
It was very discouraging.
I'm at the end of my rope.

Fortunately, help was on its way. That night, as the pyramid workers slept, Emma and Libby crept silently into their sleeping quarters. At least, that was the *plan*.

JOSHY! HI! WAKE UP, JOSHY!

The Binkertons were so thrilled to be together again, they were speechless.

They headed for the papyrus boat that the girls had hidden in the reeds. They were almost there when Libby spotted a pyramid with an open entrance.

Libby, no!

Stop her, Josh!

Sightseeing in the middle of a getaway? This was a *very* bad idea. Emma and Josh tried to lure their little sister out of the pyramid.

*Yoohoo, Libby! Would you like a nice juicy fig?*

*I'll give you a piggyback ride, Libby.*

## City of the Dead

You have probably already noticed that a pyramid doesn't just sit out in the desert all by itself. No, indeed — it's surrounded by a whole pyramid complex. This includes:

1. A valley temple where the dead king's body is received when it is brought here by boat
2. A causeway (covered road) between the valley temple and the mortuary temple
3. A mortuary temple where funeral services are performed and where food and other offerings are made
4. A low wall around the base of the pyramid
5. Small pyramids for the king's wives (sometimes)
6. Rows of mastabas where the king's family and special friends are buried after they die

The main pyramid, the smaller pyramids and the mastabas are all tombs (graves). Together, they make up a City of the Dead.

It's a nice place for a tourist like you to visit ... but you wouldn't want to live there!

But Libby had disappeared. Emma and Josh had to follow her ... into the pitch-dark tunnel.

### Inside a Pyramid

If you could see right through a pyramid, you'd find that it's mostly (but not all) solid stone. Here are some of the things you might see:

1. The core blocks on the inside. They're made of ordinary limestone. Because they're hidden underneath, they don't have to fit together perfectly.
2. The packing blocks, resting on the core blocks

3. The casing blocks on the outside. These are made of special white limestone. They're fitted together so tightly you can't even poke a hair between them.
4. The entrance to the pyramid on its north face
5. A passage leading from the entrance to the burial chamber
6. The burial chamber where the king's body is placed. Sometimes

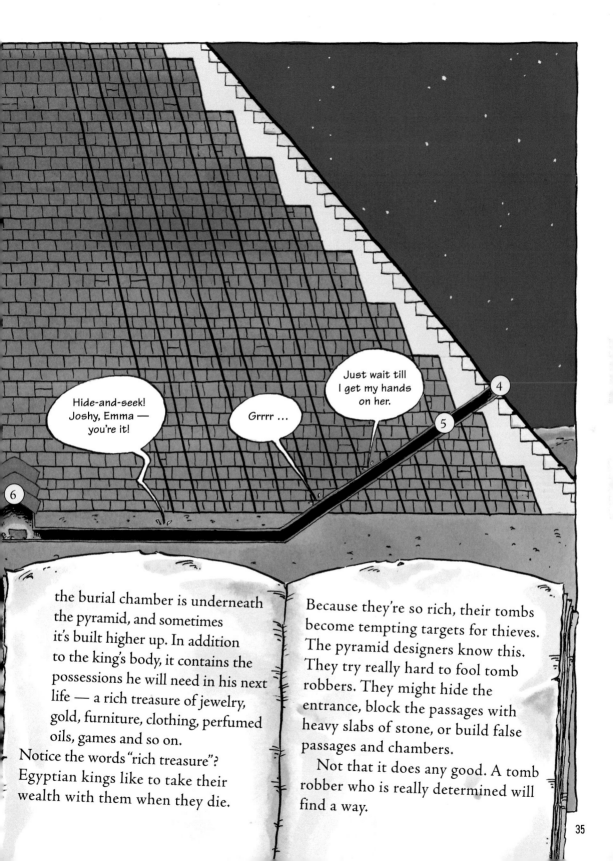

the burial chamber is underneath the pyramid, and sometimes it's built higher up. In addition to the king's body, it contains the possessions he will need in his next life — a rich treasure of jewelry, gold, furniture, clothing, perfumed oils, games and so on.

Notice the words "rich treasure"? Egyptian kings like to take their wealth with them when they die.

Because they're so rich, their tombs become tempting targets for thieves. The pyramid designers know this. They try really hard to fool tomb robbers. They might hide the entrance, block the passages with heavy slabs of stone, or build false passages and chambers.

Not that it does any good. A tomb robber who is really determined will find a way.

When the Binkertons came out into an open area, they felt relieved ... until they realized where they were.

This is a tomb, Josh.

Then that must be — ?

## How to Make a Mummy

The ancient Egyptians think it's important to preserve the body of a person who has died. They do this through a special process called mummification. It takes about seventy days, and the finished body is called a mummy.

You'll probably never have to help make a mummy — that's a job done by trained priests — but just in case, here's how:

1. Take one dead body, preferably a king. If you can't get a king, other human bodies will do — or even hawks, bulls or crocodiles. The ancient Egyptians mummified them all.

2. (Warning: This is the gruesome part.) You will have to remove the brain. (Eww! Yuck!) Stick a hooked instrument up the nose. (Ugh!) Pull the brain out bit by bit by bit. (Ick! Ick! Ick!)

3. Remove the stomach, liver,

lungs and intestines. Store them in special jars.

4. Leave the heart inside the body. The ancient Egyptians believe that the heart is where all thought and feeling happen.

5. Cover the body in a special drying powder called natron. Let it dry for forty days or so.

6. The dried-out body will have loose skin. Stuff it with padding (clay, straw, sawdust or linen) to fill it out.

7. Put sweet-smelling oils and ointments on the body.

8. Wrap the body in linen strips soaked in resin (a substance from trees). You will need hundreds of meters (yards) of these strips. Put jewels, gold and amulets in between the layers.

9. The mummy is finished. It is ready to be put in a sarcophagus (stone coffin) in its tomb, where it will stay forever … or will it?

10. Watch out for tomb robbers!

The Binkertons had really done it this time. They'd arrived in the tomb just hours after it had been robbed — and minutes before the king's guards showed up!

Once again, all the Binkertons' explanations were ignored.

Josh tried to find out what would happen to them next.

## Tomb Robbers

There is one group of people whom you should avoid at all costs in ancient Egypt. STAY AWAY FROM TOMB ROBBERS! STAY AWAY FROM OPENED TOMBS AND PYRAMIDS, TOO! They're nothing but trouble.

How will you know when you meet a tomb robber? Here are a few clues. Any greedy treasure hunter can try to rob a tomb, but certain people have a better chance. For example, the people who help to *build* a pyramid (and know about passages and so on) can come back later to rob it.

Pyramid guards sometimes let their robber buddies inside — for a price. Even temple officials can be tempted to steal the fabulous riches inside a pyramid.

So keep your eyes wide open, and stay clear of anyone who even *looks* like a tomb robber. Remember, there are serious penalties for tomb-robbing in ancient Egypt. You could be impaled on a stake. In case you're not sure what this means, let me explain: THEY WILL THROW YOU ONTO A SHARP STICK!

A word to the wise is sufficient.

At the entrance to the pyramid, the kids ran into a second group of guards who were trying to come inside. This was the Binkertons' chance!

They didn't stop running until they reached the boat.

For the rest of the night, the Binkertons traveled along the Nile. To help his sisters stay awake, Josh told Egyptian jokes.

They reached the town just as the sun rose. Emma was eager to finish reading the Guidebook so they could go home.

Unfortunately for the Binkertons, they weren't the *only* ones who had spent the night in a boat. The guards had reached the town ahead of them!

Reading while you run is generally a very bad idea — unless, of course, your life depends on it!

Emma's eyes flew over the pages as quickly as her legs flew over the ground. It was a lot for one kid to handle. In fact, it was too much.

Take it, Josh! Keep running!

Now Josh wasn't the bravest kid in all of ancient Egypt — or the strongest, or the smartest. But he was a Binkerton! And if there's one thing a Binkerton is — it's loyal. Seeing his sister fall, he skidded to a halt.

Get up, Emma! You have to!

The Binkertons ran as hard and as fast as they could ...

Read, Josh!

... but in the end ...

Faster, Josh! Read faster!

And-now-as-your-holiday-in-ancient-Egypt-dra to-a-close —

**Say Goodbye**

And now, as your holiday in ancient Egypt draws to a close, you are probably feeling many warm memories of the fascinating people you have met and the marvelous things you have seen.

Before you leave, why not take time for a final stroll through town? If you have any last-minute shopping to do, here's your chance. Or maybe you'd rather just relax and enjoy a last peaceful moment in this sun-blessed land. Close your eyes, soak up the rays ... and smell those flowers. Then it will be time to say a final goodbye to the soft, warm days and lovely, cool nights of this fabled civilization. It is an experience you will never forget for the rest of your lives.

The End

... they couldn't run fast enough.

— a-last-peaceful-moment-in-this-sun-blessed-land —

Their only chance was to *read* fast enough! Fast-enough-to-finish-the-book-and-get —

— will-never-forget-for-the-rest-of-your-lives-The —

— home!

— end!

Welcome back! Did you have a good time?

Josh was ready to give Mr. Pettigrew a piece of his mind ...

A good time? We almost got killed!

Tsk, tsk.

... but Emma and Libby just wanted to see their parents.

As the Binkertons left the Good Times Travel Agency, they swore they would never come near the place again ...

... but *never*? Well, that's a very long time.

Even for time travelers.

# ANCIENT EGYPT

## Fact or fantasy?

How much can you believe of *Hot on the Trail in Ancient Egypt?*

The Binkertons are made up. Their adventures are made up, too. So the story of the Binkertons is just that — a story.

But there *was* an ancient Egypt with mummies and papyrus and temples and pyramids and ... well, if you really want to know, read the Guidebook! That's where you'll find the facts. All the information in *Julian T. Pettigrew's Personal Guide to Ancient Egypt* is based on real historical facts about the way people lived in that time and place.

## How ancient *was* ancient Egypt?

Very! The civilization that we call ancient Egypt began more than 5000 years ago (around 3100 BCE). It lasted for more than 3000 years and left some amazing achievements, including huge pyramids that you can still visit today.

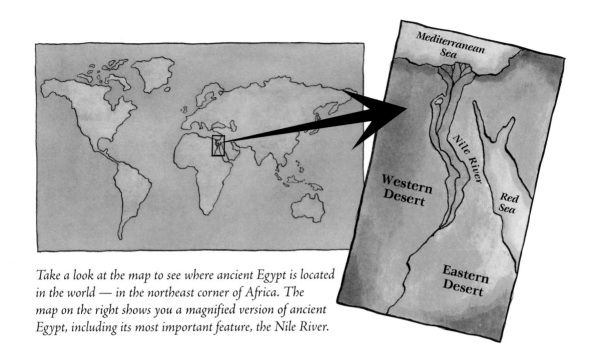

Take a look at the map to see where ancient Egypt is located in the world — in the northeast corner of Africa. The map on the right shows you a magnified version of ancient Egypt, including its most important feature, the Nile River.

## Why did a great civilization develop in ancient Egypt?

This astonishing early civilization arose in the Nile Valley in northern Africa. The people who first settled there around 5000 BCE were lucky. First of all, they had a great sunny climate. Second, they had — the Nile River! Its floods gave them rich soil, water to trap for irrigation and a long natural "road" for transportation. Basically, the Nile River provided an easy life — not easy as *you* know it perhaps, but easy for the people of that time. The Nile allowed the early Egyptians to settle down and work together to grow crops, organize communities and complete large or difficult projects.

# When did the great civilization of ancient Egypt exist?

The Binkertons' story is set around 2500 BCE, during what is known as the Old Kingdom. There were three important periods in ancient Egypt — the Old Kingdom, the Middle Kingdom and the New Kingdom. The Old Kingdom (2686 BCE to 2181 BCE) was the time when the great stone pyramids were built. It is sometimes called "the Pyramid Age." Pyramids were also built in the Middle Kingdom, but they didn't last as long. During the New Kingdom, the Egyptians buried their royals in secret tombs in a special sacred place called the Valley of the Kings.

So not *all* Egyptian kings got a pyramid. Perhaps you have heard of a famous pharoah named King Tut. He lived during the New Kingdom (long after the time of the Binkertons' visit) and was buried in the Valley of the Kings. His full name was Tutenkhamen, and he died at age nineteen. His tomb, unlike the tombs in the pyramids, was well hidden. It was left untouched for thousands of years until it was finally discovered in 1922. Inside, buried with the boy king for all that time, was a treasure trove of riches, including a solid gold coffin.

# How were the pyramids built?

*No one knows exactly how the pyramids were built.* Some remains of long, straight ramps have been found. So experts are pretty sure that ramps were used, but they don't agree on how or what kind.

Did they use a single long ramp to build the pyramids?

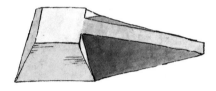

Did they use a combination of single and wrap-around ramps?

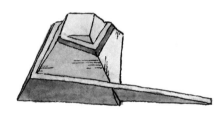

Did they use four ramps that wrapped around the pyramid, like the one Josh worked on?

No one knows for sure. New ideas and theories are suggested and tested from time to time, but the construction of the pyramids still remains one of the unsolved mysteries of the ancient world.

# How do we know about ancient Egypt?

Well, as you have just learned, there are plenty of things we *don't* know about ancient Egypt. For example, when the Binkertons were accused of tomb-robbing, they were threatened with impalement (being thrown on a sharp stick). There is evidence that impalement was used as a punishment later in ancient Egypt, but experts don't know for sure if it happened in the Old Kingdom.

Egyptologists (people who study ancient Egypt) are still learning about this ancient culture. Some of the ways they learn include: studying written records in papyrus or stone, examining ancient architecture and tombs, trying out the tools and techniques of the ancients, and digging up ancient settlements.

One such "dig" happened in the 1990s and early 2000s. In an area near the great pyramids of Giza (where some of the Binkertons' story is set), archeologists have uncovered the remains of a city of pyramid workers. This is an exciting discovery because it has provided new information about how the ancient pyramid workers lived — what they ate, where they slept, how they were treated medically and where they were buried. One surprising find was a great number of animal bones. It seems likely that pyramid workers were treated to meaty feasts!

But not all "big" discoveries are big in size. One of the most important archeological finds *ever* in Egypt was simply … a stone. It's called the Rosetta Stone and it gave us the code to the hieroglyphs. The Rosetta Stone (now in the British Museum) is a flat grey stone with the same information carved on it in three different languages — ancient Egyptian hieroglyphs, another ancient Egyptian form of writing and Greek. Before the Stone was found, people could look at hieroglyphs in Egypt all they wanted, but they had no way to *read* them. So when the Rosetta Stone was discovered in 1799, scholars got very excited. Here, finally, was a way to translate! But it wasn't till 1822 that the code was finally cracked. Since then, Egyptologists have been able to read hieroglyphs on tomb walls, temple walls, mummy cases and papyrus scrolls.

Egyptologists continue to learn more all the time. They would love to time-travel to the past and see ancient Egypt for themselves. If only they could find the right travel agency …

## For Further Exploration

### Books

*Ancient Egypt: Archaeology Unlocks the Secrets of Egypt's Past* by Jill Rubalcaba (National Geographic Investigates). National Geographic, 2007.

*Curse of the Pharaohs: My Adventures with Mummies* by Zahi A. Hawass. National Geographic, 2004.

*Egypt in Spectacular Cross-Section* by Stephen Biesty. Oxford University Press, 2005.

*Egyptian Diary: The Journal of Nakht* by Richard Platt, illustrated by David Parkins. Candlewick Press, 2005.

*Eyewitness Ancient Egypt* by George Hart. DK Publishing, 2014.

*Pharaoh's Boat* by David Weitzman. Houghton Mifflin Books for Children, 2009.

*Treasury of Egyptian Mythology: Classic Stories of Gods, Goddesses, Monsters & Mortals* by Donna Jo Napoli, illustrated by Christina Balit. National Geographic, 2013.

## Museums & Websites

Time travel is tricky! But if you're lucky, you may be able to travel one day to *modern* Egypt where you can visit the Museum of Egyptian Antiquities in Cairo, as well as famous heritage sites such as the Pyramids and the temples of ancient Thebes.

Other museums with ancient Egypt collections that you can visit in person or online include:

**The British Museum, London, U.K.**
http://www.ancientegypt.co.uk

**The Metropolitan Museum of Art, New York, U.S.A.**
http://www.metmuseum.org/metmedia/video/metkids/
　　　metkids-qanda/how-were-mummies-made
http://www.metmuseum.org/blogs/metkids/2016/ancient-egypt-game

**The Museum of Fine Arts, Boston, U.S.A.**
http://www.mfa.org/node/9457

**The Royal Ontario Museum, Toronto, Canada**
http://www.rom.on.ca/en/learn/activities/classroom/
　　　write-your-name-in-egyptian-hieroglyphs
http://www.rom.on.ca/en/learn/activities/
　　　classroom/make-a-mummy-case

### DVDs

*Building the Great Pyramid*, BBC, 2003.

*Pyramid* (hosted by David Macaulay),
PBS Home Video, 2006.

# Index